Guest Spot

CHART H

Playalong *for* Flute

WISE PUBLICATIONS
London/New York/Paris/Sydney/Copenhagen/Madrid/Tokyo

Exclusive Distributors:
Music Sales Limited
8/9 Frith Street, London W1V 5TZ, England.
Music Sales Pty Limited
120 Rothschild Avenue, Rosebery, NSW 2018, Australia.

Order No. AM955647
ISBN 0-7119-7369-5

Compiled by Nick Crispin.
Music arranged by Paul Honey.
Music processed by Enigma Music Production Services.
Cover photography by George Taylor.
Printed in the United Kingdom by Page Bros., Norwich, Norfolk.

CD produced by Paul Honey.
Instrumental solos by John Whelan.
All guitars by Arthur Dick
Engineered by Kester Sims.

Guest Spot

Fingering Guide

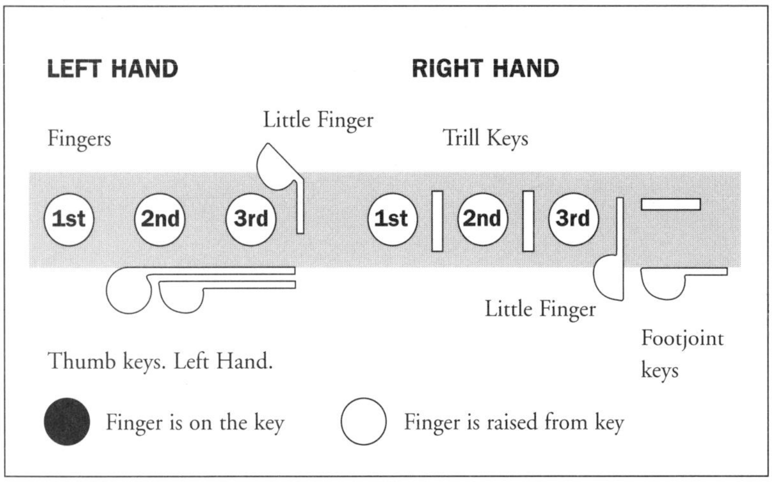

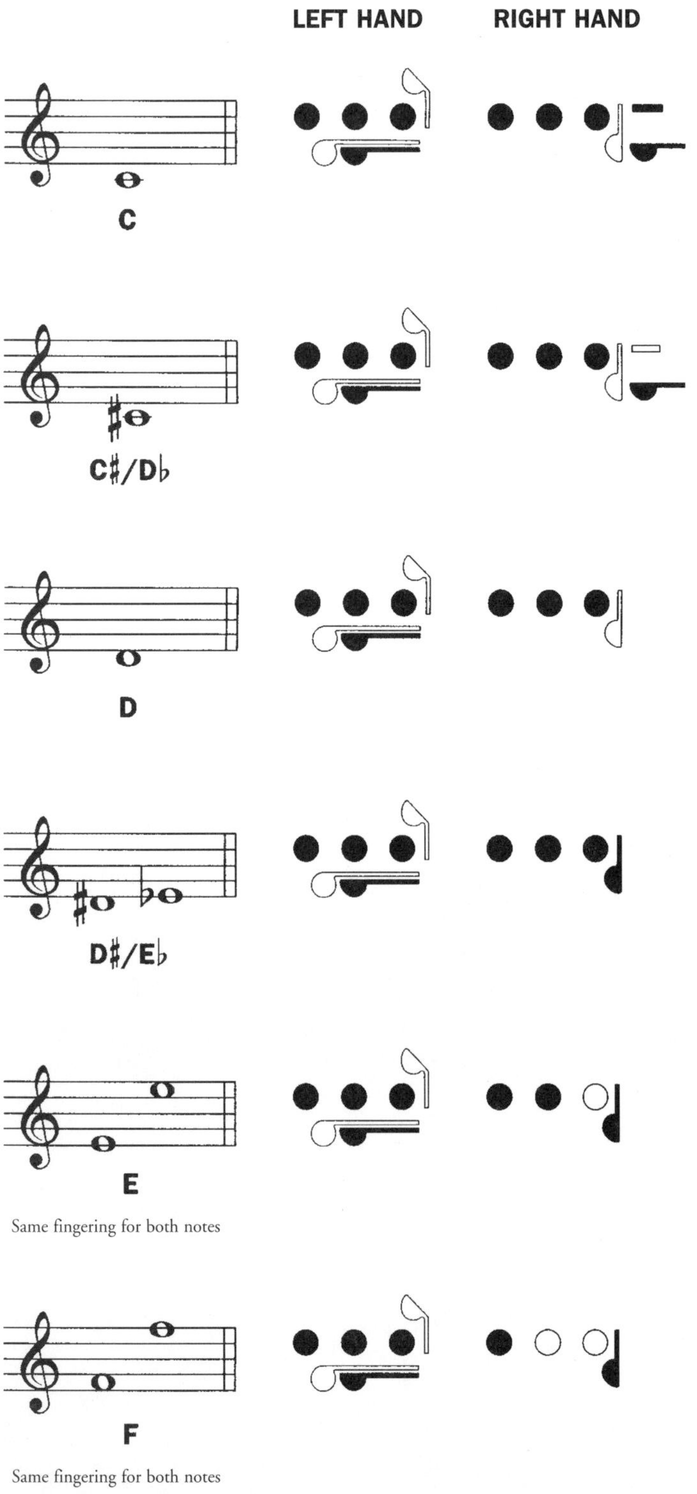

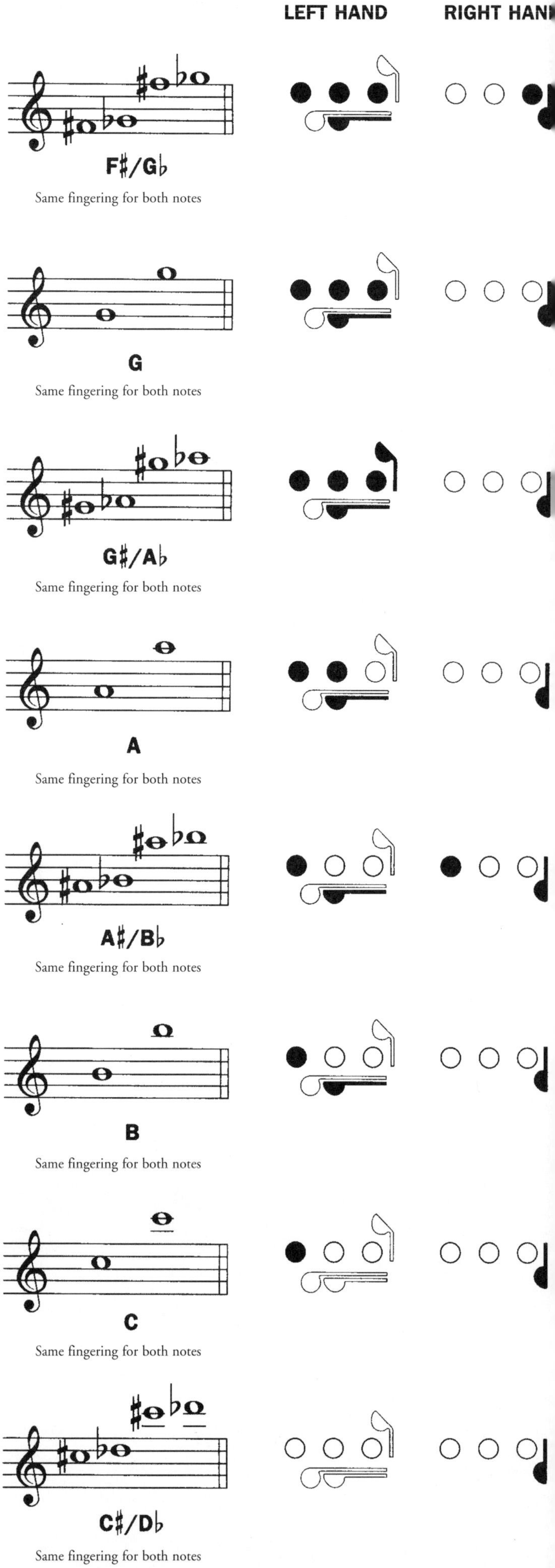

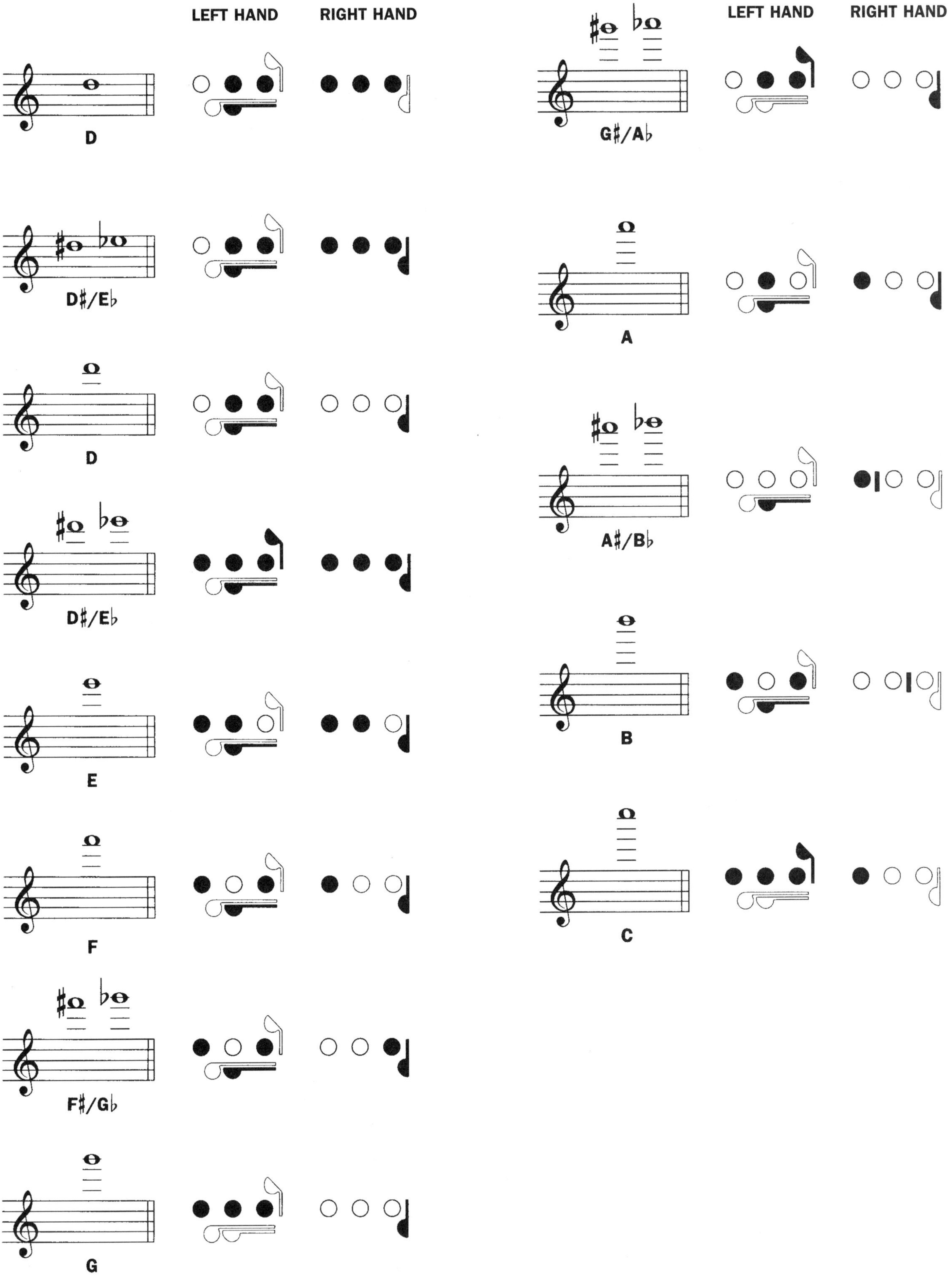
LEFT HAND
RIGHT HAND
D
D♯/E♭
D
D♯/E♭
E
F
F♯/G♭
G
LEFT HAND
RIGHT HAND
G♯/A♭
A
A♯/B♭
B
C

Baby One More Time

Words & Music by Max Martin

f
mf

f

Bring It All Back

Words & Music by Eliot Kennedy, Mike Percy, Tim Lever & S Club 7

mf
cresc.
f

Repeat to fade

Livin' La Vida Loca

Words & Music by Desmond Child & Robi Rosa

2
8

2
7

Perfect Moment

Words & Music by James Marr & Wendy Page

mp
f
mf
3
3
3
mp

Mi Chico Latino

Words & Music by Geri Halliwell, Andy Watkins & Paul Wilson

f
3

That Don't Impress Me Much

Words & Music by Shania Twain & Robert John 'Mutt' Lange

2

Repeat and fade

Tragedy

Words & Music by Barry Gibb, Robin Gibb & Maurice Gibb

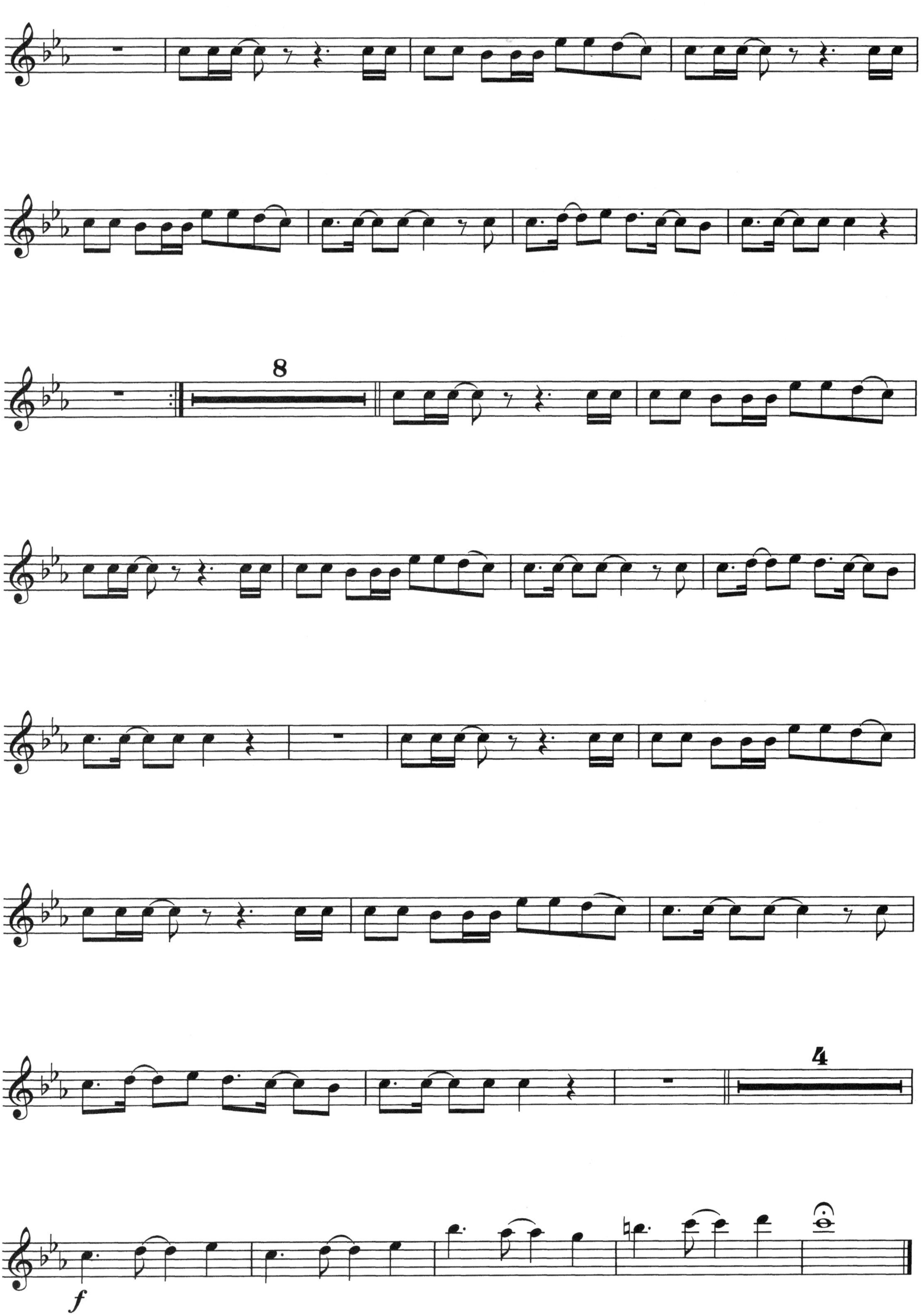
8
4
f

What Can I Do

Words & Music by Andrea Corr, Caroline Corr, Sharon Corr & Jim Corr

Moderately (swung ♪'s)

espress.
mp
Repeat to fade

When You Say Nothing At All

Words & Music by Paul Overstreet & Don Schlitz

f
mf
5
f
mf
3
Repeat and fade

When You're Gone

Words & Music by Bryan Adams & Eliot Kennedy

2/07 (61364)